ANDREW MATTHEWS
Illustrated by Tony Ross

·W·O·L·F P·I·E·

For Ben and Christopher Green

with ~~to love, there is~~ ~~d~~ never

ELM BANK

·Take·two·ripe·greedy·Monarchs·

The King and Queen were fat. Their tummies were so big that they couldn't see their feet when they walked and servants had to tell them where to step. When they sat down, pageboys had to hold up the bits of their bottoms that drooped over the chairs.

The King and Queen's subjects were thin. They wore rags and were miserable because of the high taxes they had to pay. Anyone who didn't pay was arrested by the Tax Police and locked up forever in deep, slimy pits.

The King and Queen didn't care how miserable their subjects were. All they cared about was eating new and unusual food. That was why being a Royal Chef was highly skilled, highly paid and highly dangerous.

The Royal Chefs lined up in the Throne Room and prepared to read out their menus for Royal Approval. Up stepped the Chief Chef with a nervous smile that jumped about on his face like sunlight on a duck pond.

'Your Majesties,' he said, 'today's menu begins with wart-hog tongue boiled in dolphin's milk, roasted voles stuffed with capers and toasted black beetles ...'

'Had it before!' shouted the King. 'Off to the desert with him! Stake him out where the vultures can peck him!'

Two armoured Tax Policemen clanked over to the Chief Chef and dragged him off.

'Next!' screeched the Queen.

Up stepped the Assistant Chief Chef with a smile so nervous that it shivered like a blancmange in a spin drier.

'Your Majesties, I will cook you braised walrus livers, crispy-fried elephant's trunk with bread mould, chocolate chips, candied swallows' lungs and ...'

'Had it three years ago next Thursday!' shouted the King. 'Off to Mount Disaster with him! Stake him out on the top until he freezes solid!'

'Next!' screeched the Queen.

Chef after Chef was dragged away until the moment the Queen screeched, 'Next!' and instead of a Chef, a Tax Policeman wearing black armour stepped forward.

'That's your lot, mush,' he told the King. 'There ain't a Chef left in the palace.'

'Who are you?' roared the angry King.

'Me?' replied the Policeman. 'I'm 'Arry 'Ogsflesh, Chief of Tax Police, fatso.'

'And that gives you the right to insult me, does it?'

'Yeah.'

'Oh!' said the King, relaxing. 'That's all right, then. But tell me, where is the Assistant to the Assistant Deputy Head Chef?'

'You sent 'im off to be whipped with stingin' nettles.'

'And *his* Assistant?'

'Dunked 'ead first in a barrel filled with jellyfish,' said the Policeman.

'Summon the Apprentice Chefs!' screeched the Queen.

'Keep your wig on!' said the Policeman. 'The Apprentices lost their bottle and legged it off to the forest a week ago, dog breath!'

'Scour the land!' commanded the King. 'Find me a new Chef before nightfall and I'll give you your own weight in gold!'

'Fair enough, you're on!' cried the Policeman.

·One·fresh·Woodcutter's·son· ·and·three·Wolves·

North of the palace lay a great, dark forest. In the middle of the forest stood a cosy log cabin where a Woodcutter lived with his wife and young son, Jed. The Woodcutter earned no money and so did not have to pay taxes. His was the only happy family in the land.

Young Jed had had a wonderful time growing up in the forest. He knew the names of all the plants and animals and he could hide himself, watch and listen so well he had learned the language of every forest creature.

When Jed was out alone one day, chopping up a dead tree, he heard a rustling and heavy breathing in the undergrowth behind him. He kept on chopping but listened carefully and heard the voice of a wolf saying, 'Slasher, take 'im from the right. Whitebum, take 'im from the left. I'll go for 'is throat.'

'Aw, Fang!' complained another voice. 'You always gets the good part!'

'That's because I'm bigger'n you, Whitebum. Now, ready? GO!'

The three wolves burst into the open, yelling, 'RIP 'IS LEGS OFF!'

Jed turned around, axe raised and called out in wolfspeak, 'Hold it!'

The astonished wolves stopped dead.

'The first one who comes any nearer gets my axe through his head!' Jed warned.

''Ere, Fang!' whined the wolf with a white patch on his hind-quarters. 'This geezer speaks wolf!'

'Shut up, Whitebum!'

Fang was a silvery wolf with eyes the colour of lime marmalade. 'I don't like this, lads,' he snarled. 'In the old days, it was straightforward — you met 'umans in the forest, boom, you ripped out their throats or they run off screamin'. None of this muckin' about.'

'Tell you what, Fang,' grumbled Slasher, 'I gone right off the idea of eatin' matey 'ere. When your lunch talks to you, it fair turns your insides over.'

'What now?' asked Whitebum.

Fang considered the gleaming edge of Jed's axe and said, 'Gotta negotiate.'

Depressed, Whitebum and Slasher slumped to the ground.

'It's like this, John,' Fang said to Jed. 'Me and the lads 'ere 'ave 'ad a bit of a chat, like, and we've decided that the fact you speak our language makes you sort of a special case, if you get my meanin', John.'

'My name's Jed,' said Jed, 'and I don't understand.'

'We won't rip out your throat and liver and that,' explained Fang, 'if you won't bash in our 'eads wiv your axe.'

'I second that proposal!' said Slasher.

'Vote?' called Whitebum. 'One, two, three. Unanimous!'

'Oh!' said Jed. 'In that case, anyone fancy a cheese sandwich?'

Slasher and Whitebum ate greedily and noisily. Fang was more thoughtful with his food, as though he had something on his mind. When he had licked the last crumbs from his muzzle, he said, 'Er, Jed. I been wonderin'. What do you 'umans call a bloke 'oo walks round in a white pinafore wearin' a tall white 'at shaped like a toadstool?'

'Sounds like a Chef to me,' said Jed. 'Why do you ask?'

'A bunch of 'em 'ave been stompin' round the forest all week, well lost,' Fang explained. 'They been goin' round in circles so fast it makes you feel giddy watchin' 'em.'

'Perhaps they need help,' mused Jed. 'Could you lead me to them?'

'No problem. They washes every day wiv some funny stuff that makes the water go bubbly. Gives 'em a niff like nuffink I ever smelt in all my born days!'

'Too right!' agreed Slasher. 'Can't be 'ealthy, walkin' around smellin' like that!'

'We must find them directly!' cried Jed. 'I will rescue these unfortunate Chefs and earn their undying gratitude. Lead on, noble Fang!'

'Noble?' repeated Fang. 'Knock it on the 'ead, Jed! If there's one thing I can't stand, it's a goody!'

·A· ·sprinkling· ·of· ·Apprentice· ·Chefs·

As soon as the Apprentice Chefs learned of the cruel fate that awaited them if they did not please the King and Queen, they decided to escape. Their preparations had been so rushed that they had not even had time to change and they took to their heels in full Chef's uniform.

The night they escaped, they had chosen a Pastry-cook named Adrian as their leader because he seemed less afraid of the dark than the rest of them and because he kept saying, 'We'll be all right as long as we stick together!'

So, the Apprentices stuck together, but they were not all right. Two were locked up in slime pits by the Tax

Police, four were captured by brigands, one fell in a river and five got lost. That was on the first day. At the end of a week in the great, dark forest, only ten Apprentices were left and Adrian's 'We'll be all right as long as we stick together!' sounded less and less convincing.

One lunchtime, as they all chewed miserably at roots and unripe berries in a gloomy glade, Adrian had an idea.

'Let's cheer ourselves up with a game of Hide and Seek!'

'That's how we lost Cracknell the day before yesterday,' said an Apprentice. 'In this forest there's too much hide to seek in.

Why don't we go
back to the
palace, Adrian?'

'Go back?' cried Adrian, springing to his feet. 'After all we've been through? Besides, I don't know the way.'

The Apprentices groaned despairingly.

'If you don't fancy Hide and Seek,' said Adrian, 'how about a game of I-Spy? I Spy with my little eye, something beginning with ... T.'

'Trees!' chorused the Apprentices.

'That was quick!'

'Adrian,' someone pointed out, 'when you're in the middle of a great, dark forest there isn't much besides trees that you can spy, is there?'

It was at this very moment that Jed and the wolves appeared. The Apprentice Chefs were not as grateful to

be found as Jed had imagined. In fact, their hair stood on end and they scampered up into a tree shrieking, 'The wolves! The wolves!'

'Hello there!' said Jed brightly.

'The wolves! The wolves!' shrieked the Apprentices.

'Fang,' said Jed, 'have you eaten any of these people?'

'We-ell,' admitted Fang, 'I suppose we did eat a couple, sort of.'

'What do you mean, sort of?'

'We-ell,' said Fang, 'when I say 'sort of', I sort of mean 'yes'. But we didn't enjoy 'em, did we, lads?'

''Orrible!' said Slasher.

'Stringy, like,' said Whitebum.

'Well don't eat any more!' exclaimed Jed. 'And try to look a bit more friendly. Stop slavering. You could wag your tails or even roll over to have your tummies tickled.'

'Leave it out!' gasped Fang. 'We got our dignity, you know! Wild animals, we are. Red in tooth and claw, mate! Roll over on me back? Do me a favour!'

Jed approached the tree where the Apprentices hung like worried fruit.

'Hello,' he said, waving.

'Don't listen to him, lads!' advised Adrian. 'He's a werewolf!'

'I'm not!' said Jed.

'He's a troll, then!' shouted Adrian.

'Not a very big troll, is he?' said the Apprentice sharing Adrian's branch.

Adrian peeped. 'He's a small troll! Watch out, lads, small trolls are the worst kind of trolls you can get!'

'I'm not any kind of troll,' said Jed. 'I'm just as human and normal as you are.'

'Oh, yes!' retorted Adrian. 'Strolling around with three ferocious wolves, what could be more normal than that?'

'The wolves are harmless,' said Jed.

'Harmless?' squeaked
Adrian. 'They use those dirty
great teeth to pick wild flowers, I suppose?'

'I promise they won't harm you. I'm Jed. I'm a
Woodcutter's son ...'

'A likely story!' snorted Adrian. 'What would a
Woodcutter be doing in a place like this?'

'It's a forest, Adrian,' said the Apprentice sharing his
branch. 'Where else would a Woodcutter be?'

'You all look tired and hungry,' said Jed. 'If you come with me I can give you something to eat and somewhere to rest. We don't have anything fancy, but you're welcome to share.'

He looked honest and kind and the Apprentices were fed up with being lost and frightened and hungry. They all came down from the tree, except Adrian.

'Come on, Adrian!' coaxed the others.

'Shan't!' pouted Adrian. 'You follow this kid if you like, but don't come crying to me if you get chopped up and boiled in a cauldron!'

'Won't you come too?' pleaded Jed. 'The forest can be dangerous for a solitary traveller. There are bears about at this time of year.'

'Bears?' muttered Adrian. 'Oh, all right! I'll come with you, but only to keep an eye on the others. They're such fools they'd follow any idiot!'

·A·pinch·of·Posse·

Back at the palace, Chief Tax Policeman Harry Hogsflesh had gathered a posse of his best men and two bloodhounds, Gordon and Bennett, in the Royal Courtyard.

'Right, men!' said Chief Hogsflesh. 'We got a dead important job to do and it's gotta be done before nightfall! We're goin' into the great, dark forest to 'unt down some desperate fugitives!'

''Oo's that then, Chief?' asked one of the Policemen.

'Apprentice Chefs, that's 'oo. The King and Queen are chefless, so there's no one around to fry up the Royal Grub. Our mission is to 'unt down an Apprentice and fetch 'im back 'ere.'

'Bit outside our usual line, innit, Chief?'

'Ours is not to reason why, lad!' the Chief snapped. 'It's our sworn duty, as Tax Policemen, to carry out every Royal Order without question. Besides which, there's money in it for me. We'll be ridin' through some villages on the way, so there'll be plenty of opportunity for scowlin' at peasants and tramplin' over anyone 'oo gets in our way. Mount up, men, and remember our motto — all for one and that one is Chief 'Arry 'Ogsflesh!'

·Add·one·Arrest·

Jed and Adrian were fast becoming friends. While the other Apprentices helped Jed's mother about the cabin, the two lads went out for an afternoon stroll.

In Jed's company, Adrian found the forest a less threatening place and began to dream of settling down there and opening a little inn.

A rumbling sound brought him back to the real world.

'Sounds like thunder ...'

'More like horses,' mused Jed. 'I wonder what's going on?'

His question was answered by rearing horses, shouting men, clanking armour and belling hounds. Jed

and Adrian suddenly found
themselves in the centre of
a ring of horsemen and Adrian
groaned as he recognised the
black armour of the
dreaded Tax Police Chief
Harry Hogsflesh.

'Right!' barked the Chief. 'You,' he pointed at Adrian, 'are comin' back to the palace to fill the post of Royal Chef which 'as recently fallen vacant!'

'Me?' gasped Adrian, 'But ...'

"Op up on the 'orse and let's get goin'!"

'I can't cook!' Adrian lied desperately. 'I'm a Woodcutter's son!'

'Sorry, lad,' said the Chief, shaking his head, 'your 'at is a dead giveaway. You and your assistant will 'ave to come alonger me. Rickshaw, Sedan! Dismount and shackle the prisoners! Yellowtaxi, see where the blessed blood'ounds 'ave got to!'

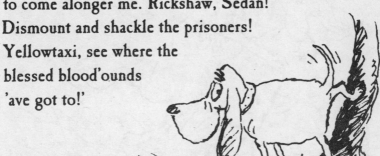

·Two·escaped·Bloodhounds·

The blessed bloodhounds, Gordon and Bennett, had run amok. There were only a few walls and posts in the palace and the sight of all the forest trees had made the dogs go starry-eyed. They had escaped in the confusion of the arrest and were happily cocking their legs over every tree in sight.

'I say, Bennett!' yelped Gordon. 'This is the life, what?'

'First rate, Gordon!' Bennett agreed. 'And have you sniffed? Heavenly! Rabbits, hedgehogs, squirrels and I don't know what else!'

'Wolves is what else, sunshine!' rasped a harsh voice.

The bloodhounds wheeled around and found themselves muzzle to muzzle with Fang, Slasher and Whitebum.

'P'raps you two'd like to explain what you're doin' on my patch,' snarled Fang.

'We're seeking political asylum,' replied Bennett.

'You what?' whined Fang.

'We're tired of the cruel regime of palace life! We want to be free to sleep beneath the starry skies!'

'Used to, like, beat you, did they?' asked Fang sympathetically.

'Goodness me, no!' Bennett chuckled at the very idea. 'They used to groom us every day.'

'Oh!' said Fang. 'Well, I 'spect they only fed you on, like, scraps an' that.'

'No, no! Liver, steak, the usual sorts of things. A servant used to bring food to the kennels in silver bowls twice a day.'

'And you'd rather live in the forest?' asked Fang.

'That's right!' barked Bennett.

'We got a right pair o' wallies 'ere!' Fang whispered to Slasher and Whitebum. He cleared his throat and said to the bloodhounds, ''Ow did you manage to escape, then?'

'Well, it's a long story,' said Bennett. 'You see, we were part of a Tax Police posse, searching for runaway Apprentice Chefs ...'

As soon as Bennett mentioned Apprentice Chefs, the wolves pricked up their ears. By the time he had reached the part of his story that dealt with the capture  of Jed and Adrian, all three wolves were growling angrily in the backs of their throats.

·One·large·measure·of·
·Royal·Bad·Mood·

The King was not in a good mood. He'd had nothing to eat all day but venison, cold pork, jelly and trifle and he'd had to part with a considerable quantity of gold.

'I'm not in a good mood,' he informed Adrian and Jed, who trembled before him in the Throne Room. 'I'm in a sort of red-hot branding iron, fingernail pulling out, ducking-stool, hanging-drawing-and-quartering-if-I-don't-get-my-way mood. And the only thing that can change that mood is a good feed of some super, extra-special, succulent dish I've never eaten before. You two will prepare that dish tomorrow for myself and the Queen. Is that clear?'

'Yes, your Majesty!' whispered Adrian and Jed.

'Off you pop, then,' commanded the King. 'Report to me with the menu tomorrow morning at eight o'clock. And remember, I'll be having the Torture Chamber aired at the same time.'

·One·newly-picked·Brilliant·Idea·

Adrian and Jed spent hours in the Royal Kitchen reading through mountains of cookbooks. Adrian racked his brains thinking of food, but when they checked, everything he could think of was mentioned in one of the fifty-eight volumes of *Collected Royal Menus*.

'It's no good, Adrian,' said Jed finally, 'we'll have to go to the King tomorrow and tell him we've tried our best but we haven't come up with anything. We'll appeal to his better nature.'

'Better nature?' wailed Adrian. 'He's the ugliest, fattest, greediest, cruellest, hardest-hearted, nastiest, most unjust and tyrannical King the world has ever seen!'

'Nobody's perfect,' said Jed.

They both jumped as a rattling sort of tap sounded at one of the Kitchen windows. It turned out to have been made by claws and when Adrian opened the window, in slunk Fang, Slasher and Whitebum.

'What are you three doing here?' cried Jed delightedly.

'Come to rescue you, ain't we?' said Fang.

'But how did you know we'd been captured? How did you know where to find us?'

'Nuffink to it!' said Fang breezily. 'See, we met these two blood'ounds in the forest and they told us as 'ow ...'

Adrian understood none of Fang's growling and yapping, but as he stared at the wolves there popped into his mind an idea so clever and daring that it made his spine ping and pong like a cold xylophone.

'I've got a really, really, really, really brilliant idea!' he yelled. 'It's the answer to everything!'

Adrian told Jed his idea and Jed told the wolves. It was really, really, really, really brilliant and it *was* the answer to everything.

·Mix·together·in·a·Royal·Audience·

At eight o'clock, the Royal Heralds burst into a flourish on their trumpets, the big double doors of the Throne Room fell open and twenty fair maidens entered, some plucking harps, some scattering rose petals.

'Well, they know how to put on a good show!' squeaked the Queen.

'Hmph! Suppose so!'
admitted the King sulkily.
Dressed in the ceremonial white
robes of a Royal Chef, Adrian swept
into the Throne Room and bowed low.
'Your Majesties!' he cried. 'You must prepare your-
selves for the most delicious, tongue-tickling delight
you have ever eaten in your lives. At lunch today, you
shall dine on ... WOLF PIE!'

'Wolf Pie!' screeched the Queen.

'Wolf Pie?' mused the King. 'Wolf Pie? Had
Horsefly Pie ... had Magpie Pie ... no ... no ... never
eaten Wolf Pie before in me life!' And at the thought of
tasting something new, his mouth began to water.

'And now,' announced Adrian, 'it is with great pleasure that I present to your Majesties, with the aid of my assistant, Jed, the main ingredient!'

And Jed walked into the
Throne Room with the
wolves, who were wearing
gold collars, muzzles and leads.
The effect was sensational.

The King and Queen went 'Ooh!' and 'Ah!' and when the wolves sat up and begged and rolled over to play dead, they applauded wildly.

'Er ... what about soups and sauces and afters?' the King enquired.

'Your Majesty,' replied Adrian, 'Wolf Pie is so completely, utterly and indescribably satisfying that no other course will be necessary. Let your Majesty imagine, for a moment, the most delicious foods he has ever eaten ...'

The table of the King's imagination groaned under the weight of roasts and stews and cakes and tarts. The thought of all that food made dribble run down his chin.

'I can see them!' he spluttered. 'I can smell them! I can taste them!'

'Your Majesty, Wolf Pie is at least a million times more delicious than any of them!'

'I must have it!' whispered the King, and then he croaked, 'I must have Wolf Pie!' and then he shouted, 'Bring me Wolf Pie!' and then he bawled out at the top of his lungs, 'PUT WOLVES IN THAT PIE OF MINE!'

·Serve·in·a·Banqueting·Hall·

At about half past ten, cooking smells wafted out of the Kitchen and filled the palace with the promise of pastry, spices, cream and meat.

The Wolf Pie was to be served at one o'clock and shortly before that time the Banqueting Hall began to fill up with guests. At five to one, the King and Queen entered, wearing their best crowns. In order to enjoy their meal more, they had eaten nothing all morning and their mouths were watering so much that servants had to follow them with mops to wipe the floor.

On the stroke of one, Adrian and Jed appeared.

'Your Majesties, my lords, ladies and gentlemen,' Adrian announced, 'Wolf Pie is served!'

The King and Queen picked up their gold knives and forks and beat upon the table, chanting, 'Wolf Pie! Wolf Pie!' The guests joined in, banging the table and rattling the cutlery and chiming the wineglasses and taking up the chant until the whole Hall throbbed with the words, 'Wolf Pie! Wolf Pie! Wolf Pie!'

Six servants came in, carrying a huge silver tray on their shoulders. On that tray gleamed a huge white dish and in the dish steamed the Pie. The sight of it stunned the Banqueting Hall into silence.

Its crust was pale gold, decorated with a forest in which wolves ran between the trees, hunted by dogs and mounted men, all made of pastry. On top of the Pie had been set a real wolf's head, eyes tightly shut, lips bared in a ferocious snarl.

The Pie was set down on the table before the bulging eyes of the King and Queen.

'Looks nice!' said the Queen.

'It looks good enough to eat!' drooled the King.

'A slight correction, your Majesty!' cried Adrian. 'It looks good enough to eat you!'

At the sound of his voice, the wolf's head on top of the Pie opened its eyes and let out a blood-freezing howl. The piecrust erupted into a fountain of pastry and fur and burning eyes and flashing teeth. Fang, Slasher and Whitebum jumped out of the Pie on to the King and Queen, howling and biting and tearing. And they ate them up, every last bit of them, until not a hair or bone or bit of gristle was left.

·Leftovers·

Not a lot more remains to be told. Everybody was tired of Kings and Queens, so free elections were held and Adrian was voted Prime Minister. He turned out to be a good one, too. He abolished taxes, got rid of the slimy pits and did a lot of other things about schools and hospitals that are a bit boring to fit into this story, but everybody in the country was really glad he did them.

Jed was offered all sorts of important jobs, but all he wanted was to get back to the forest, be a good woodcutter and learn more about animals and plants.

The wolves went back to the forest too, but they were not forgotten — the new National Flag showed three silver wolves leaping on a blue background.

And when Fang was getting on a bit, he would tell his grandchildren the tale they never tired of hearing; the story of himself, Slasher, Whitebum, Adrian, Jed and the Wolf Pie. The cubs' favourite bit was when the wolves jumped out of the Pie and ate the King and Queen.

'What did they taste like, Grandad?'

'We-ell,' Fang would say, 'I've ate a fair few 'umans in me time. Tinkers, Tailors, Teachers, Tax Policemen, Apprentice Chefs ... An' the King an' Queen tasted the same as everyone else, my son, exactly the same as everyone else!'

First published 1987
by Methuen Children's Books Ltd
Magnet edition published 1988
Reprinted 1989
Published 1989 by Mammoth
an imprint of Reed Consumer Books Ltd
Michelin House, 81 Fulham Road, London SW3 6RB
and Auckland, Melbourne, Singapore and Toronto

Reprinted 1990, 1991, 1994

Text copyright © 1987 Andrew Matthews
Illustrations copyright © 1987 Tony Ross

ISBN 0 7497 0173 0

A CIP catalogue record for this title
is available from the British Library

Printed and bound in Great Britain
by Cox & Wyman Ltd, Reading, Berkshire